Pig in the Middle

Sally Fitz-Gibbon
Illustrated by Kirsti Anne Wakelin

Fitzhenry & Whiteside

Published in Canada by Fitzhenry & Whiteside, 195 Allstate Parkway, Markham, Ontario L3R 4T8

Published in the United States by Fitzhenry & Whiteside,
121 Harvard Avenue, Suite 2, Allston, Massachusetts 02134

www.fitzhenry.ca   godwit@fitzhenry.ca

10 9 8 7 6 5 4 3 2 1

National Library of Canada Cataloguing in Publication

Fitz-Gibbon, Sally, 1949–
Pig in the middle / Sally Fitz-Gibbon ; [illustrations by] Kirsti Anne Wakelin.

ISBN 1-55041-894-7

I. Wakelin, Kirsti Anne II. Title.

PS8561.I87P53 2004   jC813'.54   C2004-901915-5

U.S. Publisher Cataloging-in-Publication Data
(Library of Congress Standards)

Fitz-Gibbon, Sally.
Pig in the middle / Sally Fitz-Gibbon ; Kirsti Anne Wakelin.—1st ed.
[32] p. : col. ill. ; cm.
Summary: A mischievous dancing pig is responsible for everything—including Grandpa!—
that disappears at Grandma's house. A girl helps her forgetful grandparents solve
the mystery as they learn to accept their befuddled state.
ISBN 1-55041-894-7
1. Pigs—Fiction—Juvenile literature. 2. Grandparents—Fiction—Juvenile literature.
3. Memory—Fiction—Juvenile literature. I. Wakelin, Kirsti Anne. I. Title.
[E] dc22 PZ7.F589Pi 2004

Fitzhenry & Whiteside acknowledges with thanks the Canada Council for the Arts,
the Government of Canada through the Book Publishing Industry Development Program (BPIDP),
and the Ontario Arts Council for their support of our publishing program.

Design by Fortunato Design Inc.

Printed in Hong Kong

In memory of
my father and my grandparents
—Sally

In memory of
my great-grandparents and my grandpa
—Kirsti

Sometimes Grandma has a problem.
Sometimes the pig dances in her garden.
That's when Grandma needs my help.

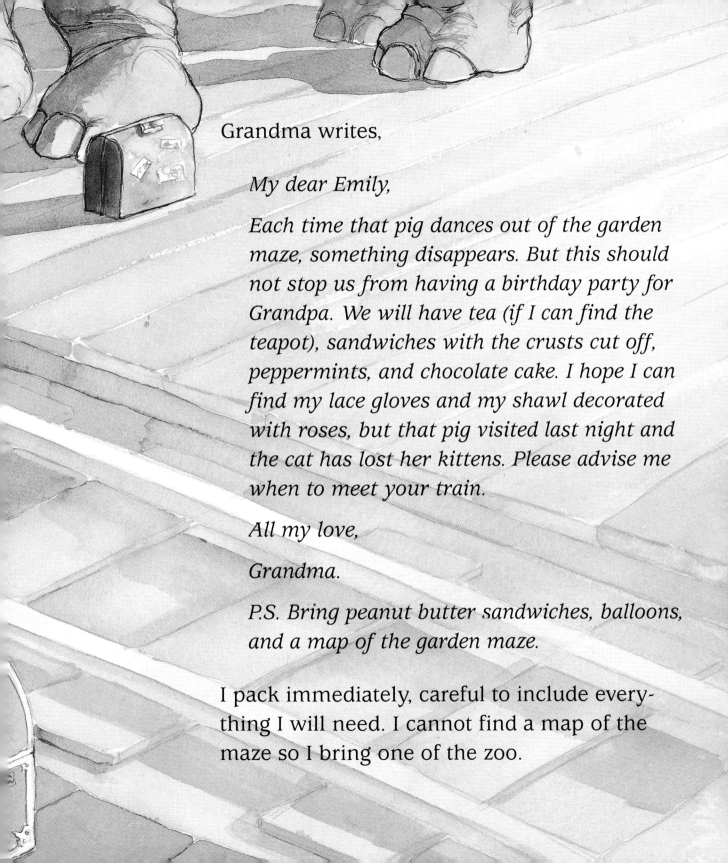

Grandma writes,

My dear Emily,

Each time that pig dances out of the garden maze, something disappears. But this should not stop us from having a birthday party for Grandpa. We will have tea (if I can find the teapot), sandwiches with the crusts cut off, peppermints, and chocolate cake. I hope I can find my lace gloves and my shawl decorated with roses, but that pig visited last night and the cat has lost her kittens. Please advise me when to meet your train.

All my love,

Grandma.

P.S. Bring peanut butter sandwiches, balloons, and a map of the garden maze.

I pack immediately, careful to include everything I will need. I cannot find a map of the maze so I bring one of the zoo.

Other than a slight problem with the balloons, my trip is uneventful.

Grandma meets me at the station and we load everything into her car.

It is bedtime when we reach my grandparents' house. Grandpa is nowhere to be seen. The dog meets us at the door. He looks worried.

"Wear these earmuffs," says Grandma. "The pig sings while she dances. Ignore her. We will get ready for the party first thing tomorrow morning."

But even the earmuffs don't keep out the noise. Sleep is impossible, so I climb out of bed and go to the window. Music and fireworks are coming from the maze. I can hear laughing and singing.

I go back to bed, but not before I see a small pig twirling through the roses with my grandpa. They are both laughing as they dance their way into the maze.

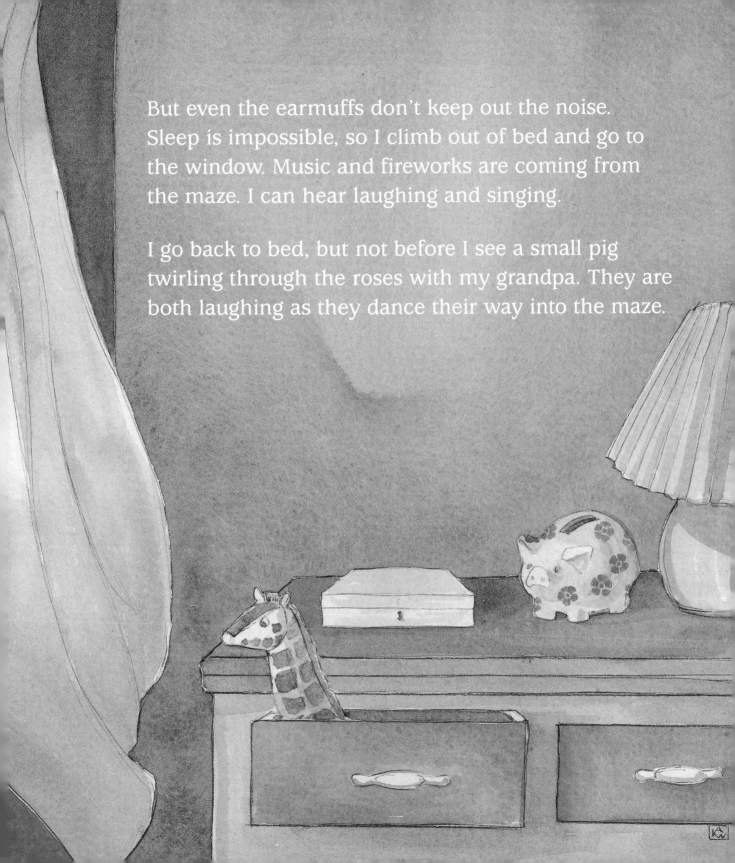

At breakfast the next morning, I announce, "Grandpa is gone."

"Oh, dear," says my grandma. "There are little pig footprints all through my kitchen."

She can't find the toaster so we eat some of the peanut butter sandwiches.

"I don't like the look of this," I say to Grandma.

"Neither do I," she replies. "The pig usually cleans up after herself."

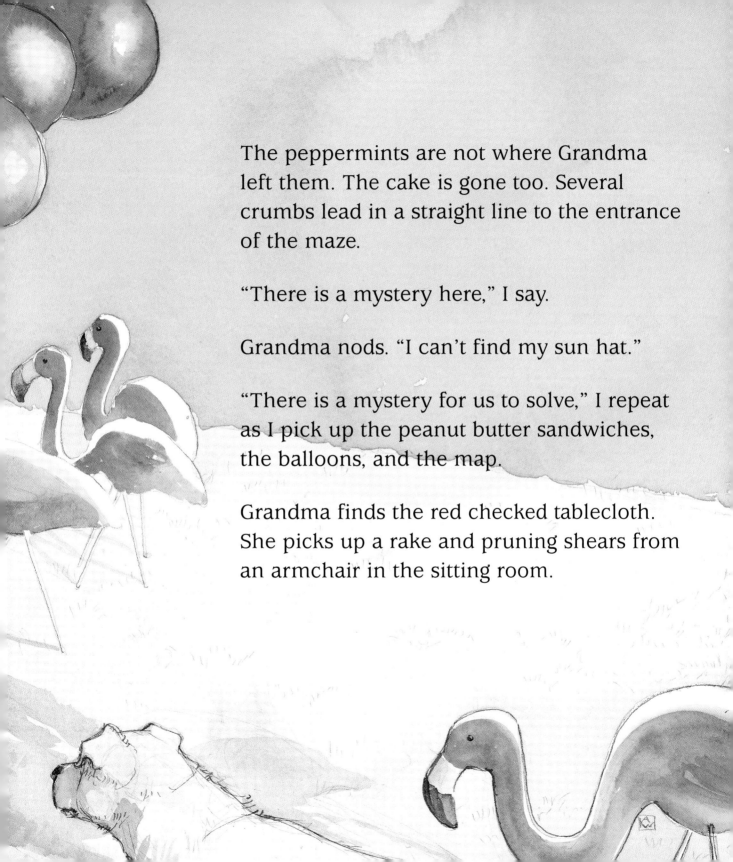

The peppermints are not where Grandma left them. The cake is gone too. Several crumbs lead in a straight line to the entrance of the maze.

"There is a mystery here," I say.

Grandma nods. "I can't find my sun hat."

"There is a mystery for us to solve," I repeat as I pick up the peanut butter sandwiches, the balloons, and the map.

Grandma finds the red checked tablecloth. She picks up a rake and pruning shears from an armchair in the sitting room.

I lead the way to the maze.

I tie a balloon to the entrance so we can find our way out.

At first we can't find the way in, but Grandma waves the tools around until the bushes open up.

Almost at once I discover evidence.

The cat disappears at the first dead-end.

Very soon we are hopelessly lost.
The zoo map is no help at all.

After struggling along a difficult path,
we come to a note that reads:

> *If you are this far, you may as well stop
> for lunch. If you aren't here yet, you had
> better keep walking. The party will not
> start until much later.*
>
> *Signed,*
>
> *Portia Pig.*

Some things begin to show up as we sit on
the grass.

We shake the crumbs off the tablecloth.

I read the map again. "If there is any trouble, you can wave the rake. We can tie another balloon here so that we know where we have been."

Grandma nods and clips a branch off the maze as a warning that we will not stand for any more nonsense.

We are thirsty by the time we find the teapot. Someone has left it full of tea, so we stop again.

"I think we must be getting close, now," whispers Grandma. "I can hear your grandpa snoring. I would know that sound anywhere."

We lose sight of the dog.

We push our way around a corner and see… Grandpa!

Grandpa wakes up with a start and asks for a balloon.

"Why, you are just in time for the party," says the pig.

We leave the balloons tied to the maze in case we need them again.

And then we all go home.